To Elias &
Malachi,

Have fun with Phoebe!

Miss Hulett

Hey guys!

We camped next to the author when we were in Florida. Such a neat person. Enjoy the story about Phoebe!

Love Grandma and Grandpa Reames

Published by
Possum Publishing
251 Fry Terrance SE
Port Charlotte Florida 33952

Printed in the United States by Grandville Printing, Grandville, Michigan
First Edition
ISBN 978-0-692-79310-7

Phoebe Flies Away

An Adventures of Phoebe The Possum Book

Written by Janis Murphy and Miriam Hulett

Illustrated by Stefanie St. Denis

My name is Phoebe, and I'm a 'possum. When I was born, I was just a little bigger than a honey bee.

1

I crawled into
my mother's pouch to
grow some more. After I grew
bigger, I rode on my mother's back.

My family lived in the woods in a hole in a tree. My mother would use her sharp claws to climb down the tree to find food. She ate things like bugs, nuts or fruit. Sometimes she hunted for mice or snakes.

3

We lived close to a family that had a big dog named Rufus. One day when we were big enough to wander away from our mother a little, Rufus had gotten out of his yard. My mother called us, warning us of danger.

She called and called, but I had wandered too far and couldn't find her. So I hid in the stump of an old tree. When I thought it was safe to come out, I went looking for her.

I looked everywhere for her, but I couldn't find her.

I was lost and alone and afraid. I lay down in
the soft grass and cried and cried.

The lady who owned Rufus had come into the woods to get him. She heard me crying. She picked me up and cuddled me. Her hair smelled good and she had soft, smooth skin.

The lady took me home and gave me a warm bottle of milk
with honey in it. She was very gentle and talked to me
in a soft, loving voice. I started to feel better.

She let me sleep with her, and she would sing softly until I drifted into *sleepyland*. Every few hours I would wake up. Then she would give me more milk and sing me back to sleep.

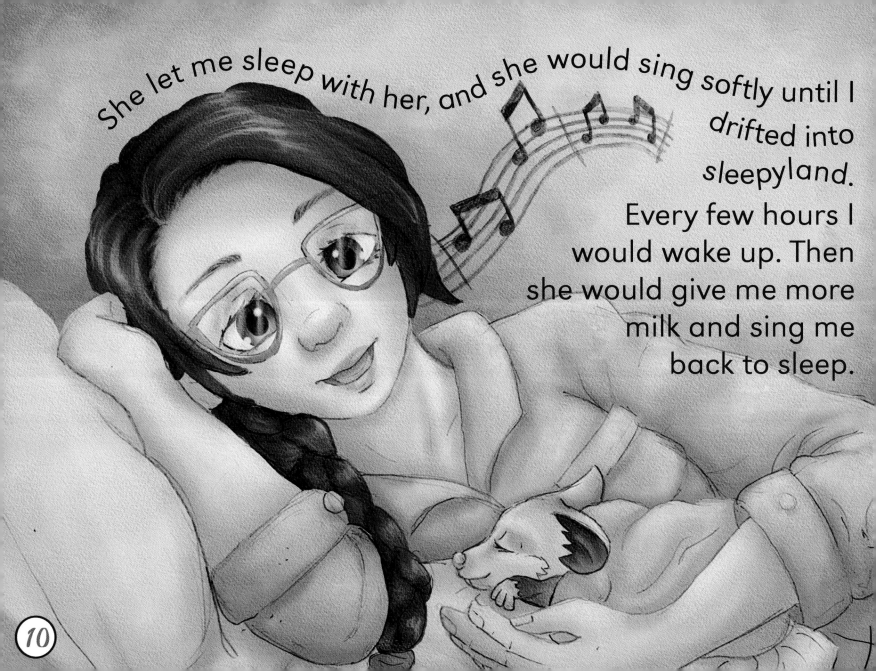

Soon I grew big enough to eat other food. I really liked chicken and grapes.

The lady carried me around with her and let me sleep in her collar.

Sometimes I would climb up into her hair and fall asleep. 'Possums love to hang onto their mother's fur and go for rides. So this was fun for me. Rufus became my friend, so I could ride on his back too. I liked playing with Rufus.

The lady and I did lots of fun things together. Once we took a trip on an airplane. I rode along inside her collar.

When we rode in the airplane, we went into a big building.
I heard the lady call it an airport. The trip was fun.
I rode everywhere in the ladies collar.

We visited lots of places. My favorites were the Washington Monument and the National Zoo where we saw lots of strange animals. The lady said we were in Washington D.C.

15

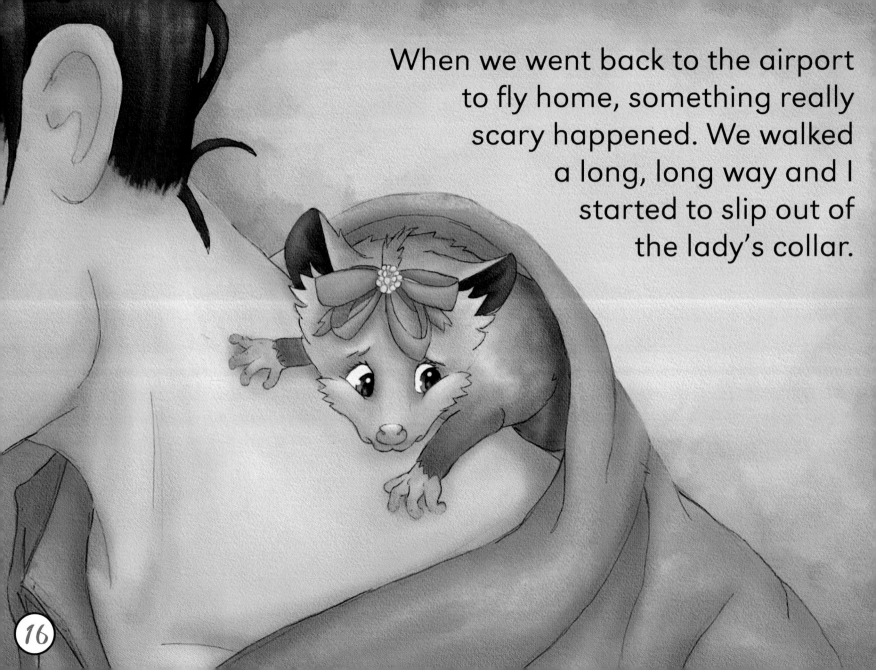

When we went back to the airport to fly home, something really scary happened. We walked a long, long way and I started to slip out of the lady's collar.

Next thing I knew, I was
falling down, down, down.
I was so scared! I bumped my
head when I hit the floor.
Boy did that hurt!

17

I heard a man say "Hey lady, you dropped something." I looked up to see all these people standing around me.

Some of them were pointing at me.
Some of them were laughing.
It hurt my feelings when
they laughed at me.

All at once I looked up and there was the lady. I sure was glad to see her. The lady picked me up and put me back in her collar. It was warm and snuggly, and I felt safe again.

I liked flying in the airplane. I liked all the things we saw. It was fun going on the trip with the lady, but it can be really scary to get lost like I did.

If you go on a trip, have fun and be sure to stay close to your family.